Kitten Friends™ #6

Patch the Perfect Kitten

by Jenny Dale
illustrated by Susan Hellard

Aladdin Paperbacks
New York   London   Toronto   Sydney   Singapore

Look for these KITTEN FRIENDS books!

Special thanks to Gwyneth Rees

To Magnus and Hattie, and

in memory of Matilda—three perfect cats.

First Aladdin Paperbacks edition June 2001
Text copyright © 2000 by Working Partners, Limited
Illustrations copyright © 2000 by Susan Hellard
First published 2000 by Macmillan Children's Books U.K.
Created by Working Partners, Limited

Aladdin Paperbacks
An imprint of Simon & Schuster Children's Publishing Division
1230 Avenue of the Americas
New York, NY 10020

4 6 8 10 9 7 5 3

Library of Congress Catalog Card Number: 2001089678
ISBN 0-689-84031-4

Chapter One

"Let me out!" the kitten meowed from deep inside a large, wet cardboard box. She nuzzled the lid to try to open it.

The box had been dumped at someone's front door, and for the past hour the wind and the rain had been steadily falling on it. The tiny kitten was becoming very wet, very cold, and very frightened. "Help!!!" she yowled again, and this time it was so loud that the box around her almost shook.

A door opened, and a strange voice said, "What was that noise?" Suddenly the box was opened, and a girl's face looked inside. The kitten trembled and desperately tried to hide in the corner.

"Oh, you poor thing!" said the girl as she carried the box inside the house, where her parents were getting break-fast ready. Twenty bowls of cat food took quite a long time to prepare, so her mom and dad were very busy indeed.

"Now, what have you got there, Louise?" Mrs. Dodds, her mother, asked.

"Someone left a kitten outside the front door. It looks *so* cold and frightened!"

Louise carefully lifted the tiny, bedraggled kitten out of the box and cuddled it close to try to warm it up.

"What a scrawny little thing! It doesn't look very old." Mrs. Dodds examined the kitten more closely. "It's a girl. She looks

like she could do with a big breakfast."

Hearing the word "breakfast," the kitten meowed hungrily and tried to wriggle out of Louise's arms to reach the tasty dish of cat food Mrs. Dodds was holding in her hand.

"Better take her into the clinic and warm her up first," Louise's mother said, stroking the little kitten on the top of her head. "I'll be there in a minute. I'll bring some water and some food."

"Oh, Mom! Can't we keep her here in the house?" Louise begged.

"Now, Louise! You know the rules! We have to check all newcomers out before they can mix with the other cats. The vet's coming this morning, so we can get your new friend seen right away."

Reluctantly, Louise did as she was told.

As she carried the kitten back out into the hall, she looked up at Louise for the first time. Two bright green eyes, round and blinking, fixed on her, and then the kitten gave a little meow and started to squirm as the front door loomed closer.

She meowed, trying to bury her head in Louise's woolly sweater.

"Don't worry. Soon you'll be nice and warm," Louise reassured her, opening another door and carrying her into the clinic. She gently set the kitten down on the shiny metal table and went to get a clean blanket.

The kitten, left all on her own, meowed again sadly.

Another, louder meow greeted her from a large cage, where a plump gray kitten with amber-colored eyes was curled up, inspecting her. "Don't worry, she'll be back in a minute," the bigger kitten said. "So how did *you* end up here? You don't look too good. . . ." He yawned politely. "Still . . . I suppose they must be expecting you to live, or else they'd be making more of a fuss."

"Of course I'm going to live!" the younger kitten meowed. *Although if someone doesn't bring me breakfast soon, I might not make it,* she worried. In her last home, the people often went to work

and forgot to feed her in the morning.

"So how *did* you get here, then?" the gray kitten asked again.

"I was left outside this house, and a young girl called Louise found me."

"Ooh, you were lucky! *My* last owners tried to drown me, but I was rescued. My name's Oscar, by the way. This place is all right. They'll find you a new home, that's for sure. I'm leaving just as soon as I've seen the vet."

"The vet?"

"That's right," Oscar said. "He's the person who makes sure you're fit and healthy. He looks a little frightening, but he's really not so bad. Hey, I'd stop scratching if I were you. They'll think you've got fleas! Maybe you *have* got fleas! If you do, don't come near me. I've just gotten rid of mine!"

The little kitten started to tremble. She remembered her last home and someone shouting at her:

"*FLEAS!* SHE'S FULL OF *FLEAS!* I TOLD YOU WE SHOULDN'T HAVE

GOT HER! SHE'S GOING STRAIGHT TO THAT CATS' HOME UP THE ROAD, THAT'S WHERE SHE'S HEADED!"

The kitten meowed miserably. She was sure she'd be sent away again just as soon as everyone found out she had fleas. People didn't like fleas, but then kittens didn't like them, either. It was horrible to be nipped at all day long. Kittens hate having those itchy pests in their nice coats.

"Here you are!" Louise called out, coming back into the room with a warm blanket. The little kitten was shivering as she wrapped her in it. "Hey, there's no need to be frightened. I'm not going to let anyone hurt you."

Louise stroked her head and laughed. "You're going to have a lovely tortoise-shell coat soon. Now, what shall we call you? What do you think, Oscar?" Louise asked the other kitten. "Shall we call her Patch, since she's so patchy all over?"

Oscar blinked his large amber eyes and looked at Patch's scrawny coat. It was so grubby that Oscar didn't see how Louise could tell what color it was going to be. Oscar twitched his nose in Patch's direction to try to get a sniff of her. Oscar hoped Patch didn't smell as bad as she looked, especially if they were going to put her in the empty cage next to his.

"Well, Patch seems to be a reasonable

description of her, I suppose," Oscar meowed to no one in particular.

"Well, I like it!" Patch replied. "It's much better than the name my old owners gave me."

As Louise cuddled her, Patch wanted to warn her about the fleas because she didn't want them biting Louise, too. So she told her about them in the only way she knew how: She reached under her chin with her back paw and scratched at her neck vigorously.

"Oh, dear!" Louise said, sighing. "We'd better ask the vet to give you something to get rid of those nasty fleas. Don't worry. Soon you won't be itchy at all. You really are a beautiful kitten, Patch!

We'll find a home for you in no time, and until we do I'm going to look after you myself!" She sat down with Patch on her lap and turned Patch over on her back so she could tickle her tummy.

Patch had never had her tummy

tickled before. And it had been a long time since she had made the funny noise she was making now. It was a sound that seemed to be coming from her chest and causing her whole body to tremble. And it was so loud!

"Don't worry!" Oscar called back to her cheerfully. "You're purring, that's all. It just means you're happy."

Patch realized that she *was* happy. And the more Louise stroked her and talked to her, the happier she felt.

When Louise's mom came in a few minutes later with a big bowl of cat food, Patch felt even happier!

Chapter Two

"I've put some chopped meat on top this morning as a special treat," Mrs. Dodds said as she handed Louise a bowl of food for Patch.

It had now been several days since that first morning when the vet had given her an injection in the scruff of her neck and sprayed nasty-smelling liquid all over her, which made her fur tingle.

Patch hadn't enjoyed seeing the vet one bit, but luckily her fleas hadn't, either. They'd all disappeared and hadn't come back since!

No one had ever given her fresh meat before, and she had to ask Oscar what it was.

"It's chicken," Oscar said, his nose twitching at the smell of it. "Most cats can't stand it. Bring it over here and I'll eat it for you if you like."

Since the chicken smelled so tasty, Patch decided to try a piece, anyway. And she was delighted she did! "I *like* chicken" she meowed excitedly to Oscar. "I'll be happy to eat all of *yours*, if you don't like it!"

But for some reason, instead of being pleased, Oscar seemed quite huffy. He went to lay down with his back to Patch and started to chew his claws. His tail was swishing as if he was upset.

"Oscar, you've already had some

chicken this morning!" Louise said, laughing, which made Oscar's tail swish even more.

"Louise, there's a young couple with a little boy coming to look for a kitten tonight," Mrs. Dodds said, carrying a bucket and mop toward Patch's cage. "Why don't you give Patch a good comb when you get home from school? Try to pretty her up a bit?"

Louise didn't reply. Patch noticed she had stopped smiling.

"Oh, Louise," her mom said briskly. "Don't look at me like that. You know we can't keep Patch. If we kept all the kittens that got handed in to us, we'd have hundreds by now!"

"But I don't want to keep *all* the kittens," Louise murmured. "I just want to keep Patch!" She couldn't explain why Patch was special to her. She just was.

But as it happened when the young couple came, they walked straight past Patch and picked a white kitten, who had come in the day before. Patch was glad to see that kitten go. Every time Patch had tried to be friendly toward her, the white kitten had just ignored Patch as if she smelled funny.

The following week, after Louise had gone to school, Patch and Oscar were allowed in the kitchen while Mrs. Dodds was cleaning out their cages. Patch had never been in a kitchen before. She thought it looked very exciting.

"Now, no scratching anywhere but here!" Mrs. Dodds said, firmly tapping the scratching post as she set it down in one corner.

"Where else would we scratch?" Patch asked, looking around after Mrs. Dodds had gone. The kitchen had a wooden floor with no bits of scratchy carpet in sight.

"She means here!" Oscar said, demonstrating how well he could sharpen his claws on one of the big wooden table legs. "And here!" He bounded over to some bumpy wallpaper next to the refrigerator. Soon he was so excited that his tail bushed up. He began to race around the kitchen, leaping up onto chairs and down again and into the litter box and out, sending litter flying everywhere as Patch watched.

Patch wanted to play, too. She was just wiggling her bottom, ready to pounce on Oscar, when Oscar leaped up onto the kitchen table out of reach. As Patch jumped up to join him, the kitchen door opened.

"PATCH!" Mrs. Dodds shouted angrily.

Patch looked down in confusion at Oscar, who had jumped down as the door opened and was now sitting innocently licking one paw.

"PATCH!" Mrs. Dodds yelled again. "GET DOWN!"

Patch jumped down quickly. She hated being shouted at. Luckily, at that moment, the doorbell rang, and Mrs. Dodds went to answer it.

"They don't like cats on the table," Oscar explained. "Next time you'll have to jump down more quickly when you see them coming." He straightened his paws out in front of him and gave a long stretch, followed by a yawn. "I hope the house I'm going to live in has a nice, warm fire. If it does, I'm going to lie down right in front of it all day long. It's going to be purrr-fect!"

"They might not have the fire on all

day long!" Patch said, feeling a little sad. She always felt upset when Oscar boasted about his new home, because she knew she didn't *have* a home yet. Well, not one where she could get to stay forever and ever.

"I hear that old ladies always have their fires on all day long," Oscar said smugly. "And they give you lots of milk— even though the vet says it's not good for you." Oscar licked his lips at the thought. "I got picked right away! When it comes to choosing kittens, people always go for the cute ones first."

Just then Louise's mom came back into the room with an elderly lady close behind her.

"Here's your new mom, Oscar," Mrs. Dodds said, picking him up.

"Mrs. Smith, I don't suppose you want *two* kittens to keep you company, do you? This is Patch, and she needs a good home, too!"

Patch held her breath because Oscar wasn't looking too pleased. Patch felt pretty sure that Oscar had set his heart on being an only cat.

"Well, aren't you a pretty girl?" Mrs. Smith said, smiling at Patch.

"Yes, she is *now*," Mrs. Dodds agreed proudly. "But you should have seen the state she was in when she first arrived!"

Mrs. Smith thanked Mrs. Dodds for offering, but she could only manage one kitten. So the last that Patch saw of Oscar was a final swish of his gray tail as Mrs. Smith popped him into her cat basket. But she couldn't stop thinking about what Mrs. Smith had said. *Pretty*, she had called her. No one but Louise had ever called her *that* before!

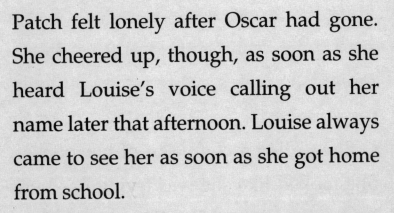

Chapter Three

Patch felt lonely after Oscar had gone. She cheered up, though, as soon as she heard Louise's voice calling out her name later that afternoon. Louise always came to see her as soon as she got home from school.

"Patch, don't be sad! We'll soon find a nice home for you, too," Louise comforted her, sitting down on the floor and pulling her onto her lap. Louise had a way of stroking Patch in just the right places— under her chin and behind her ears and right on her forehead above her nose— so that she soon felt happy and purry again. If only she could stay curled up on Louise's lap forever. . . .

But just as she was thinking that, Louise said, in a shaky voice, "Some people are coming to look for a kitten tonight, so we've got to have you looking your best."

She pulled a comb out of her pocket. She looked like she was trying hard not to cry. "I wish you didn't have to go!"

Patch didn't want Louise to be sad. She knocked the comb out of Louise's

hand and jumped up onto her shoulder to rub her face against hers.

"Patch, stop it! Your whiskers really tickle!" Louise smiled, sounding braver as she reached up to grab her. "Come on. Let's get you ready! Dad says that Mr. and Mrs. Ferguson have a nice big house with a huge garden. There'll be lots of trees for you to climb, and loads of other cats around to play with. You're going to really like it!"

That evening Mr. and Mrs. Ferguson arrived at the cats' home in a red sports car, which made a lot of noise as it pulled up. Louise went to the window to look at them as they walked up the front path. They were young and well-dressed.

The man walked very quickly around all the cat cages, as though he was in a terrible rush.

"We haven't got much time," his wife, Clare, explained. "We have a dinner party to go to tonight. Oh, look!" she exclaimed, stopping outside Patch's cage. "Isn't this one *so* cute?"

Patch did her best *not* to look cute by sticking her leg in the air and licking it the way she had seen the grown-up cats do. She always thought it made *them* look pretty silly.

"Look at the way she's cleaning herself! Isn't she sweet?" Clare said.

Patch stopped licking her leg and curled up in her box at the back of the cage, with her back to the young couple. Maybe if she showed them how sulky she could be, they'd go away.

"Oh, how cute! She's such a shy little darling!"

"Well, if she's too shy to make mischief,

then that'll suit us fine!" Clare's husband said briskly. "We've just moved into a brand-new house, with all new furniture. In fact, she's the same color as the living room carpet!"

Clare gave a silly giggle and said, "Here, pretty puss!" to Patch, who made a face and started to scratch her ear. What she wouldn't give now for a good dose of fleas!

"The vet's checkd her out. She's all ready to go," Louise's dad said.

"Fine. We'll get the cat basket from the car."

Louise was frowning as they hurried out. "You shouldn't pick a kitten just because it matches your carpet!" she said angrily.

Her father smiled. "I expect they were just joking." He became more serious when he realized how sad Louise felt. "Sweetheart, you know we can't keep Patch here."

"I never said that! I just don't want her to go somewhere where . . . she'll get stepped on all the time because they can't tell the difference between her and their silly carpet!"

"Louise, now come on!" her father said, putting his arm around her. "You'll make Patch nervous if you act like this. Why don't you give her a chance to see if she likes her new home? Wouldn't that be best?"

So Louise gave Patch a final cuddle

and tried to pretend she was pleased for her as her new owners came back carrying their brand-new bright pink cat basket. "Be good, Patch!" she said as she put him inside.

"Patch?" Clare said, curling up her nose when they got to the car.

"Oh no, we'll give you a much more distinguished name than that, my precious!" She poked her long, painted fingernails into Patch's basket and wiggled them about. "What about Gertrude?"

"But I *like* the name I have!" Patch meowed indignantly. Of course she didn't want to change it. Louise had given it to her. She meowed that she wanted to be taken back to Louise immediately!

"She's got such a dear little meow, hasn't she, darling?" Clare cooed. "She's just *so perfect.*"

Patch stopped meowing abruptly. What was it Oscar had said to her about her meow? "You have to practice sounding pathetic when *you* want a saucer of milk! You have a naturally pathetic little mew! Some dotty old lady is going to spoil you rotten if you play your cards right!"

Patch didn't want to be spoiled by a dotty old lady—or a dotty *young* lady like the one who was calling her a cutie-pie as they drove away. She just wanted Louise.

Patch took a big breath and filled her lungs with as much air as possible. Then she gave the loudest, most ear-piercing meow she had ever shrieked in her life. That was just for starters. By the time Patch had meowed as loud as she could for the whole ride back, her new owners were raising their voices in order to hear each other.

"She'd better be house-trained!" Clare's husband shouted at her. "If not, we're taking her straight back!"

"House-trained? Of course I'm house-trained," Patch was about to tell them, when suddenly she had a much better idea!

Chapter Four

Patch inspected the carpet in her new home. It was true that she blended in remarkably well with it. It was multi-colored—a mixture of brown and black and orange and white—just like Patch. And it had a nice feel when Patch dug her claws into it.

"Stop that, Gertrude!" Clare shrieked. "Here!" she said, plonking a scratching post down in front of Patch's nose. Patch immediately ran under the table.

The table had wooden legs like the one in Mrs. Dodds's kitchen, but these legs were polished and had delicately carved feet at the bottom.

Patch decided to try her claws out on one of them. The wallpaper in this room looked quite promising, too—not nearly as old and tattty as the stuff in Louise's kitchen, but it would do.

"GERTRUDE!" Clare screamed at her.

Patch ignored her. After all, *her* name wasn't Gertrude, was it? Her name was Patch!

"Patch!" Louise cried out excitedly the

next day as she spotted her back in her cage when she got home from school. "What are you doing here?" Then she spotted her mother, who wasn't looking quite so pleased.

"Mr. Ferguson brought her back this afternoon. He said they couldn't cope with her behavior. I can't understand it. Patch was always such a perfect kitten when she was here with us."

"She still *is* perfect!" Louise said, opening the door of Patch's cage and picking her up to cuddle her. Patch was purring loudly. "What did Patch do, Mom?" She stroked Patch's head as she put her down on the ground again.

"Apparently she acted like she'd never

seen a scratching post before in her life,"
Louise's mother said, sighing. "*Or* a litter
box!"

"Oh, dear." Louise frowned at Patch,
who was pretending to be very inter-
ested in a piece of fluff on the floor.

"Let's just hope someone else comes along soon," Mrs. Dodds said. "Although I'm not sure the Fergusons were suited for a cat."

"Yes," Louise said bravely. "Let's hope somebody really *nice* comes along soon."

But this time Patch really wasn't listening. She had spotted a spider and she was trying to tap it with her paw. By the time she had finished playing with it, Louise had gone away. Patch hoped she wasn't annoyed with her. She was just glad to be back near Louise again, that was all, and she wanted to tell her that. She knew Louise would come to see her again before she went to bed because she always did.

But that night she didn't. Louise's father came to check on her instead. "The sooner we get you out of here, the better, Patch," he said gently, stroking her on her back.

"Where's Louise?" she meowed anxiously. Surely Louise wasn't so annoyed with her that she didn't love her anymore. She felt so upset just thinking about it that she couldn't get to sleep. When she finally did, she had a horrible dream about Louise shouting at her and calling her a bad kitten.

"Oh, Patch!" Louise said, and for a moment Patch thought she was still dreaming until she opened her eyes and saw Louise crouching down beside her holding her bowl of breakfast.

Patch jumped up and rubbed her head against Louise.

"Oh, Patch, I'm sorry I didn't come to say good night last night, but Mom and Dad think I'm getting too attached to you," Louise said. "Do you understand?

They think that the more time I spend with you, the harder it's going to be for me to give you up again."

Patch didn't really understand. All she understood was that she felt happy again because Louise wasn't upset with her. And Louise was tickling her under her chin just the way she liked best.

"Now, listen, Patch," Louise whispered. "There's a really nice old man, Mr. Hedley, who is coming to look for a kitten. Dad's already told him all about you. He sounds very kind, and he wants a cat to ease his loneliness because he lives all by himself."

Patch gave her a look that said, "Why can't I just stay here with you?" but

Louise either didn't understand or was pretending she didn't, to avoid having to give Patch an answer.

Later, when Mr. Hedley came to take Patch home with him, Louise was nowhere in sight. Patch gave a little whimper as they put her inside a cozy box with a warm blanket. She sat very quietly the whole way home on the bus. The old man talked to her in a kind voice. He reassured her that he wouldn't be upset if Patch was naughty. But Patch didn't feel like she had the energy to be naughty. Besides, what good would it do? She'd never see Louise again, anyway. . . .

Chapter Five

Louise felt too sad to do anything after Patch left. She sat in her bedroom all alone. She even ignored the telephone when it rang, even though she knew her mom and dad were both busy feeding the cats. But the phone kept ringing, and when Louise's dad finally answered it, Louise's heart gave a little leap.

"Well, if that's the case, then of course

you must bring her back," Mr. Dodds was saying.

Is it Patch? Louise wondered, racing down the stairs as her dad hung up the phone. "Is Patch coming back again?"

Mr. Dodds shook his head. "That was Mrs. Smith. Her daughter wants her to go live with her, and she can't have a cat there. So she's bringing Oscar back tomorrow."

"Oh no, poor Oscar," Louise murmured. She had never felt as close to Oscar as she had to Patch. For one thing, she had always felt that Oscar didn't like her petting him and picking him up as much as Patch did. But she made up her mind to give him lots of affection to make up for losing his home with Mrs. Smith.

Oscar arrived back looking very upset. Mrs. Smith looked so sad as she gave him one last cuddle.

Oscar started meowing loudly in protest.

"He'll settle down again after a while," Louise's dad said, and pretty soon Oscar did. At least, he stopped being noisy and went to sleep in his basket. In his dreams he was still lying on Mrs. Smith's rug in front of the fire waiting for teatime, when he would have fresh boiled chicken and a saucer of milk all to himself.

When Oscar woke up, Louise brought him some of his favorite chicken-flavored cat food, but he just sniffed at it and turned his head away.

"Oh, dear. We're both down in the dumps, aren't we?" Louise said, sighing. "You miss Mrs. Smith, and I miss Patch. Let's just hope that Patch isn't feeling as sad as we are."

* * *

Two days later, Louise was upstairs doing her homework when the doorbell rang. She heard her mom go answer it. Then she heard a voice she recognized, so she ran downstairs to see what was happening.

Mr. Hedley was standing in their hallway carrying a large cardboard box.

"She hasn't been naughty," Mr. Hedley was saying as he handed the box to Louise's mom. "She's just been so sad that I couldn't bear it any longer. She hasn't eaten anything. I couldn't even tempt her with some fresh chicken."

Louise rushed over to the box and cried out, "Patch!"

A loud meow answered her. A few moments later Louise was holding Patch in her arms, and she was purring frantically as she rubbed her head against Louise's chest.

"Oh, so you *can* purr!" Mr. Hedley said, smiling.

Mrs. Dodds was shaking her head in disbelief as she watched the fuss Patch and Louise were making over each other.

"It seems that Patch has already found his perfect owner!" Mr. Hedley added, his eyes twinkling as he looked on. He glanced mischievously at Louise's mom. "Don't you agree, Mrs. Dodds?"

Chapter Six

Louise couldn't stop smiling after her mom finally agreed that she could keep Patch.

Mr. Hedley was smiling, too, but he sounded a bit sad as he stroked Patch good-bye and said, "I expect I'm too old to think about giving a home to a young kitten."

Suddenly Louise had an idea. She

looked at her mom.

Louise led the way to Oscar's cage, where he was lying curled up with his back to them, pretending to be asleep.

"Oscar!" Patch cried out excitedly, and when Louise opened the door of the cage, she leaped out of her arms and scampered over to tell Oscar that she was back—and for good!

But Oscar, who was in a very bad mood indeed, snarled, "Leave me alone!"

"Someone's feeling sorry for herself, eh, puss?" a kind, elderly voice said.

Oscar rudely hid his face under one paw.

Patch started to describe how old Mr. Hedley had a log fire and had tried to tempt her with fresh chicken and chopped liver and a saucer of egg yolk.

"Egg yolk?" Oscar sniffed. "Liver?" His mouth was beginning to water.

"That's right!" Patch said.

"Oscar isn't himself at all since he had

to leave Mrs. Smith's," Mrs. Dodds was explaining.

"Normally he's much more mischievous than this." She smiled. "Although he thinks we don't know that."

"Mischievous, eh?" Mr. Hedley was reaching down to stroke him. "Well, that sounds just right for me. I like mischievous kittens."

Oscar sniffed the old man's hands. He liked the smell of them. He stood up and licked them. They tasted good, too, almost as good as old Mrs. Smith's after she'd been chopping up chicken for him.

Oscar suddenly felt very hungry. He felt so hungry, he thought he could eat a whole chicken! He decided that Mr.

Hedley might make a good owner after a bit of training, and he rubbed his head against him to tell him so. He also wanted to let Patch know that Mr. Hedley was *his* property now!

"Well, it looks like we've got two

perfect kittens belonging to two perfect owners," Mrs. Dodds said, laughing.

Both Patch and Oscar disagreed. *They* thought it was more a case of two perfect owners belonging to two perfect kittens, but they didn't say anything. It was just too difficult to purr and talk at the same time!

Everyone needs Kitten Friends™!

Fluffy and fun, purry and huggable, what could be more perfect than a kitten?

by
Jenny Dale

#1 Felix the Fluffy Kitten
0-689-84108-6 $3.99

#2 Bob the Bouncy Kitten
0-689-84109-4 $3.99

#3 Star the Snowy Kitten
0-689-84110-8 $3.99

#4 Nell the Naughty Kitten
0-689-84029-2 $3.99

#5 Leo the Lucky Kitten
0-689-84030-6 $3.99

#6 Patch the Perfect Kitten
0-689-84031-4 $3.99

Everyone needs Puppy Friends™!

Bouncy and cute, furry and huggable, what could be more perfect than a puppy?

by
Jenny Dale

#1 Gus the Greedy Puppy
0-689-83423-3 $3.99

#2 Lily the Lost Puppy
0-689-83404-7 $3.99

#3 Spot the Sporty Puppy
0-689-83424-1 $3.99

#4 Lenny the Lazy Puppy
0-689-83552-3 $3.99

#5 Max the Muddy Puppy
0-689-83553-1 $3.99

#6 Billy the Brave Puppy
0-689-83554-X $3.99

#7 Nipper the Noisy Puppy
0-689-83974-X $3.99

ALADDIN PAPERBACKS
Simon & Schuster Children's Publishing
www.SimonSaysKids.com

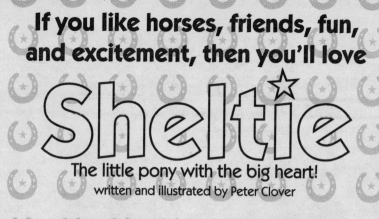
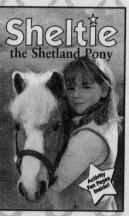

Read all of the
Aladdin Angelwings
stories!